THIS BOOK BELONGS TO

____

Made in the USA
Monee, IL
11 April 2021

65521294R00063